Caught
IN THE
Shower
GAY EROTICA

NICCI HAYDON

Contents

Caught in the Shower

By Nicci Haydon

Print Edition

Copyright 2018 Nicci Haydon
All rights reserved

This is a work of fiction. Names, characters, businesses, places, events and incidents are either the products of the author's imagination or used in a fictitious manner. Any resemblance to actual persons, living or dead, or actual events is purely coincidental.

Chapter 1

Ed

Coren must have thought he was there alone.

After all, usually the apartment was empty on a Thursday evening, when I was out at football practice and Hugh had date night with Amelia. But that night, football was cancelled.

The light spilled out from the bathroom into the hall, and it was a complete accident when I spotted him. The hiss from the shower almost drowned out his terrible rendition of I Will Survive. I chuckled a little to myself, thinking of how Hugh would rip into him for that one.

Yes, clearly Coren thought he was alone.

I had never seen my roommate naked before. Soap bubbles hung like a mane around his shoulders as the water cascaded over his head, down the curve of his back, over muscular buttocks that shifted up and down as he twisted and turned. Short dark hair was plastered to his scalp, a tattoo of a wolf on his left shoulder blade shifting and puckering as he lathered himself.

The door was only open a crack, just enough to let the steam escape into the hall. I thought about heading back to my room, but I was frozen in place.

"Something something that mad look in outer space..." Coren tried to whistle the tune but the water got into his mouth and he just spat it against the glass panel, then sighed, rubbing soap into his hair.

I bit my lip as I watched, my erection growing, partly because I'd never noticed before just how good looking Coren was, but also partly because of the situation. Watching him shower, unexpected, unintended. I'd never had those kind of thoughts about other men before, but I can appreciate a sexy moment when I'm in one.

Coren let out a moan, then turned, eyes closed, letting the water hit his back and giving me a full frontal view.

And it was magnificent.

I already knew that Coren was a bit of a health freak, of course. Me and Hugh had never tempted him with a slice of pizza or a sneaky Friday night takeaway. But all those salads and smoothies must be high in protein because he was sculpted. I mean, like a bodybuilder. Wide, thick pectorals seemed to hang from his shoulders. Below them, his abs were just slightly mismatched, so that those on the left sat higher than those on the right. And they all pointed down to a crotch shaved clean of hair.

And there, between his legs, his cock swung lazily.

It was soft, but still big. My mouth was dry as I watched it bounce with his movements, the bulbous head visibly shaping the foreskin, a couple of veins twisting and winding along the topside.

I shifted from one foot to the other, sure I should stop watching now even as the bulge in my pants grew firm and uncomfortable. Coren ran a soapy hand down, over his abs, and massaged his crotch, cock and balls rolling through his fingers.

My mouth dropped open as I watched him play, watched him stroke his soft length. My cock swelled with need as I imagined myself touching Coren, making him moan. I knew that I should go, that I should stop watching, but I couldn't.

Then, without warning, a high-pitched squeak escaped my lips.

Chapter 2

Ed

Coren's eyes snapped open, and they fell right on me.

All of a sudden, I felt light headed, like I might faint at any moment. I wanted to say something, make some excuse, but my brain couldn't focus. Every muscle in my body was screaming to turn and run, to run as fast as I could and never come back to the apartment.

But every one of them was frozen in place.

"Hey, man." A smile tugged at the corner of Coren's lips. He didn't stop what he was doing, didn't try to hide his crotch with his hand as he stroked his cock. "What's up?"

The way he emphasised the word 'up' made me shiver. My mind raced back and forth between the urge to flee and the...what...invitation?

"Come on, Ed, stop looking so worried. You just want to stand there, that's cool." His eyes pointedly lowered, and my cock jumped up another inch in response. "Or you could join me." I watched as his fingers pinched the head of his cock and he drew in a sharp breath.

"No." I muttered, shaking my head. "No, I'm not..." I couldn't even say the word. After all, if he was then I didn't have a problem with it, right? It's just that I wasn't.

Coren laughed. "Ed, it's cool. Whatever." He bit his lip and closed his eyes, a short moan echoing against the bathroom tiles. Then he sighed, eyes still closed, and almost moaned the next words. "Nobody's saying you're gay. I'm not gay. But you like sex, don't you? I know I do. It's just more fun with two."

Fuck, I was hard. The way that Coren talked, it was like there was no shame in how my body was reacting at the sight of him. And we were both single. I mean, nobody was going to get hurt here.

"Oh, man, you have no idea how good this feels." His cock was covered in soap bubbles, slick and silky as his hand gripped it tight, sliding down the length as it hardened, the head stretching the

4

foreskin back. "At least come in here to watch, so I know you're not going to run away."

I had to make a decision. More than anything, I still felt embarrassed about just standing there in the hall while he masturbated. I could just leave, though, right? Just go back to my room. Sure, there'd be some awkwardness between us for a day or so, but it wouldn't last.

But I couldn't even turn my head. I was into this. Absently, my hand dropped to my crotch, trying to shift my erection into a more comfortable position inside my jeans.

Something about that touch broke the spell. Feeling how hard I was at this, how much I obviously enjoyed what was happening. And Coren had said it was OK, after all.

I pushed open the bathroom door and stepped inside, leaving it wide so that the cooler air from the hall could rush in as I leaned against the opposite wall and finally allowed myself to just enjoy the moment. Coren's cock was darkening with blood as it grew harder still, the head engorging, swelling, as his fingers popped over it and he sighed and moaned, steam swirling around his toned body.

And without any judgement, I slid my hand inside my pants.

Chapter 3

Ed

I let out a long sigh as my fingers finally ran along the length of my shaft, stimulating the sensitive nerves as I watched Coren tossing himself off. Fuck, it felt good. The head of my cock was swollen and I squeezed it gently between my thumb and forefinger, moaning and half closing my eyes as the blood was forced back.

"Feels good, right?" Coren grinned, teeth showing, then raised his arms above his head, leaned back and stretched under the running water.

I nodded. "I can't believe we're doing this."

"Are you kidding, man? I can't believe we haven't done this before!"

Coren laughed, abdominal muscles straining, tensing, making sharp angles over his skin. I didn't even bother hiding my interest any more. I watched, mouth slightly agape as the water splashed and sputtered against his naked flesh, steam lazily drifting around his body. I stroked myself as I watched, my erection so painfully coiled inside my pants that I groaned and gritted my teeth, but didn't want to stop.

"Why don't you take your clothes off, Ed? It's not like you've got anything I haven't seen before."

I didn't respond straight away. I mean, he was right. If we were in the locker room at the gym I wouldn't think twice about stripping down in front of him. Of course, I wouldn't have a raging hard-on, but then neither would he.

"Well..."

He laughed. "That's a yes, man, just go for it." He made a cross over his chest as he said, "I swear this stays between us."

What could I do? I wanted to be naked. I wanted to have the room to just masturbate while I watched him. And the idea of him watching me... well, Jesus Christ, that made my heart flutter and my stomach clench. It terrified me and I wanted it more than I wanted my next breath.

Barely able to believe what I was doing, I unbuttoned my pants, then lowered the zipper. Coren didn't look away, but he didn't stare either. He just watched with interest. As I pulled down my pants, I found myself still trying to shift my body in such a way that it would hide my embarrassment. Was I really such a prude? I'd never thought so before. With a deep breath, I forced myself to stand up straight, my boxers tenting over my cock, rubbing against the head and sending a burst of sensation up my spine, right into my brain.

"Hey, you've got nothing to be embarrassed about there," Coren said, grinning. "You're hung."

I smiled and shrugged, not sure what I could say to that. Should I return the compliment? No, that would just be awkward. "Thanks," I said, then hooked my thumbs under the waistband of my shorts and slipped them down fast before I lost my nerve.

Coren licked his lips, then started stroking himself again with one hand, while his back moved up and down against the shower wall, his other hand hooked over the glass above his head. He didn't look away from me. He gazed at my cock and slowly licked his lips as his hand moved up and down his shaft.

Nervously, I reached down and slipped my hand over my cock, drawing in a sharp breath as it jumped up in response. I swear I was never this hard with women. Never this sensitive to every touch, every breeze through the open door.

"Ed, man, this water feels fantastic," Coren said, leaning his head back and letting the warm water fill his mouth, then spitting it out. "Stay there if you want, but there is enough space in here for two."

Chapter 4

Ed

I smiled, trying to process what Coren had just said. Was he actually asking me to join him? "I...I don't think so," I said, cupping a hand over my cock. This whole thing was a mistake. I mean, I no longer even remembered why I had gone out into the hall in the first place. It was my fault that I was watching him, but that was really only for a second or two.

Coren shrugged. "Suit yourself. But the water is divine." He rolled his head under the shower jet, breath coming long and slow as the steam swirled. His hand, unlike mine, simply moved up and down, up and down along his shaft, squeezing the head of his cock gently as his ball sack swung beneath. "Come on and go, get out the door, don't you come back now any more..." I cringed as he started singing again.

I leaned back against the bathroom wall, closing my eyes. My cock was still as hard as rock, and a single hand was doing nothing to hide it. I let my fingers drift over the head, swirling around the tip, as my wrist brushed against the hem of my T-shirt. God, it was sticking to my skin, the mixture of sweat and steam making it stifling.

"Oh, fuck, man, you're missing out. The heat from the water and the blood in my cock. It's amazing."

My eyes drifted open. I couldn't help it. Coren was right there, just turning under the jet of water, stroking himself without any trace of self-consciousness. He seemed so free, and I still felt like the dirty little perv, watching and...

With a sigh, I dragged the T-shirt over my head and tossed it to the floor, then stepped closer to the shower. "Still room for two?"

Coren didn't even open his eyes. His lips curled in a half smile. "Of course, step in."

Gingerly, careful to keep my cock from brushing his skin, I stepped into the shower. There was enough room for two, but apart from the spray that bounced off Coren's skin I couldn't get right under the water. Instead, I stood there awkwardly, too afraid to-

"You afraid I'm going to bite or something, Ed?"

I laughed, "No, it's just..."

"Man, we get closer than this when we're watching TV together. Come on, who cares if your skin touches mine? It's only skin. Think of it like shaking hands."

He shifted over, just an inch, but it was enough to make the invitation clear. I was nervous, this was the first time I'd done anything like this, but I think a part of me was also excited. It was taboo, different, maybe even socially dangerous. I slid in beside Coren, thighs and shoulders brushing against each other. The water rushed against the top of my head, ran down my neck, over my back. Coren turned my way and his cock slid against my waist.

"You want to borrow my shower gel?"

What could I say? "Er, sure, thanks."

He grabbed it and passed it to me, and didn't bother to look away as I squirted a little onto my hand and started to rub it into my skin. Bubbles lathered in my chest hair, spilled down my stomach to my crotch, caught on the top of my erect cock. Instinctively, I reached down, rubbed the soap over my stomach, then hesitated.

"You missed a spot," Coren said, grinning.

What possessed me in that moment, I can't honestly say. Coren was taller than me, more muscular than me. Something about that made me feel playful. I smirked as I reached down between us, smoothed the bubbles along the top of my shaft, drawing in a deep, hitching breath as I did.

And then I turned my hand, and smoothed those same bubbles along Coren's cock.

Chapter 5

Ed

Coren's teeth sunk into his bottom lip, his eyes boring into my own. "Now that's interesting," he said, a slight grin curling the side of his mouth. "I think somebody's feeling playful."

I felt my face go red. What the fuck? Instinctively, I pulled my hand away-

Coren's fingers caught my wrist. "Uh-uh, no you don't."

I opened my mouth to protest, but no words would come out. He pushed my hand down, towards my own crotch, and I hardly resisted at all. "What are we doing?"

"Whatever you want to do."

He winked, licking his lips, and then looked down pointedly. And I swear I couldn't help it. I swear it was an involuntary spasm. My cock jerked upwards, and I let out a moan as a jolt of sensation buzzed through my brain.

When my palm brushed against the tip of my cock, I wanted to speak, wanted to tell him to stop. Instead I closed my eyes, cupped my hand over the head and swirled my palm over the hypersensitive skin, my back arching against the wall as my legs went weak.

"You like that?" Coren's voice was a distant, half-heard murmur, but I nodded.

"Mmm."

"Can I touch?"

God, that thought almost blew my mind, almost made me blow my load. I felt the blood rush to my crotch, engorging the head of my cock against my hand. I imagined Coren's skin against mine, imagined him tentatively stroking a finger along the underside of my cock as I swirled my hand over the end.

Just the fact that he had asked so politely, despite everything that was happening...

I nodded my head, then tensed in anticipation.

When his fingers touched my balls, I lifted up on tip-toes, sound squeaking through my lips. Maybe I had no idea just how sensitive I would be to his touch, maybe I had expected him to go straight for my shaft. Whatever it was, the feeling of vulnerability just made me harder. He took one of my balls between his thumb and forefinger, gently squeezing, rolling it in his fingertips, and I bleated, barely able to catch my breath.

"How does it feel?"

I nodded, squirming under the hot water. "Good. Fuck, Coren, I've never-"

"Just relax and enjoy."

He squeezed again. It was gentle, but just enough to put me on the edge of pain. Damn, it was unexpected. And oh my god, I would never have thought it could be so hot. His fingers trailed up the underside of my shaft, the back of his hand brushing against my own as I continued to swirl my palm over the head of my cock, then suddenly his voice was closer, his breath warm on my face as he spoke.

"Can I kiss you?"

I nodded. "I'd like that."

The feeling of his lips against mine drowned out the whole world. They weren't soft like a woman's lips. They were harder, somehow, more intense. Still warm, but different. I relaxed into the kiss, my body dropping down from tip-toes as he stroked me, as I stroked myself. I was lost, enjoying everything, not knowing or caring what this all meant, only aware that it was fun, it was easy, there was no judgement between us-

"Well, this looks cosy!"

My eyes snapped open and I pulled away. My heart was still thundering, my cock was still engorged and ready. But my head suddenly felt light.

There, in the bathroom doorway, stood Hugh and Amelia. And they were both grinning like satisfied cats.

Chapter 6

Amelia

Ed's face. Oh my God, if I only had a camera in that moment I would have taken a photo just to show him what he looked like. Mind you, a photo of that scene would have kept me warm and relaxed all night, I can tell you. And Coren, the little slut, he knew exactly what he was doing.

No shame, that one.

I shook my head as Coren grinned at me, trying to keep a straight, disapproving face, but quickly losing the battle. As I inclined my head, snorting out a laugh, Hugh made his feelings very clear.

"What the hell, you guys? I'm gone for one evening and this happens?"

"Hugh, look, I don't know what..."

That was the last straw. Ed trying to explain the situation just had me in stitches. What was he going to say? It wasn't what it looked like? I mean, come on, how could it be anything else?

Even as the tears started rolling down my cheeks though, I felt bad. What if they'd walked in on me and my room-mate Sophia in a compromising position like that? Yeah, I wouldn't have been pleased.

I clasped a hand on Hugh's shoulder. "Don't be mean," I said, wiping away tears with my free hand as I turned to Ed. His cock was still so hard, dripping with soap bubbles... quite, quite tempting... "Ed, seriously." I forced my eyes up to his face. "You have absolutely nothing to be ashamed of. We're all friends here. It's nothing I haven't seen before. Next time though, might be a good idea to close the bathroom door. We'll go." I squeezed Hugh's shoulder. "Come on, let's leave them to it."

"Oh." Coren sounded disappointed, and I turned a hard stare on him.

"You are a bad boy."

"Yes, but..."

Hugh and I had been together for almost a year, but Coren had been my best friend since high school and I'd known Ed for years. It was Coren who introduced me and Hugh, and Coren who offered Hugh a room when his tenancy agreement ran out. I knew full well that he didn't really see any difference between sex with women and sex with men.

I was also aware that he fancied the pants off Ed. I mean, Coren isn't the kind of person to keep things to himself. No details are spared. I know all about his masturbatory thoughts, and they're not even remotely clean.

"No, Coren," I said, firmly. "This is between the two of you."

"Three," he said, and I shook my head.

"No! I'm not staying."

"Not you, Amelia. Him." He turned his eyes towards Hugh. "Can't you see how much he wants to be in here?"

When I looked at Hugh, his eyes went wide and he shook his head.

"I don't!"

"Oh, come on." Coren sounded bored. "You don't mind, do you, Ed?"

I honestly didn't know where to look. Coren was right, it was written all over Hugh's face. His bright red face. He was shaking his head still, but I could tell. When I raised my eyebrows and turned my head to think, there was Coren absently pulling on Ed's cock while turning him gently under the steaming water.

And boy was it hot.

Unconsciously, I raised a hand to my nipple and brushed a palm over it, felt how hard it was under the thin fabric of my top. I so wanted to masturbate right then.

"If you want to, then say you want to," I said to Hugh. "It's not illegal or anything."

"No way, I'd never cheat on you."

"And if I said it was OK?"

He opened his mouth to speak, then hesitated, and I could see the thoughts processing through his head. Oh God, I wanted him to say yes. Jesus Christ, the thought of the three of them right there...

"Are you saying that?"

"Only if I can watch..."

Coren's yip of delight was matched by a low moan from Ed, and Hugh slowly nodded.

Chapter 7

Hugh

I kept my eyes on Amelia as I pulled my shirt up over my head. I mean, this felt weird, I wasn't going to deny it. Every part of my logical brain was telling me she wouldn't be OK with this, that I'd see a flicker of something else cross her face as I stripped. Trouble was, my logical brain wasn't the driving force in that moment.

She reached out a finger and ran it between my pecs, down my stomach. It made me shiver and gasp a short breath. My body wasn't quite what it used to be, certainly not like Coren's, and I wondered what was going through her mind. She was friends with Coren long before I came along. Had they ever...

Pushing the thought out of my mind, I leaned in for a kiss and she accepted it with a smirk.

"So, what, are you going to shower with your trousers on?"

She glanced down and my already throbbing cock engorged just a little more. The idea of her watching me...watching us...shit. I took a deep breath, hoping none of them noticed how nervous I was at that moment.

Coren snorted a laugh. "If you're not quick, man, we'll be done before you even get a look in."

To my surprise, Amelia started fumbling with my belt. To my greater surprise, I didn't even try to stop her.

The buckle slid aside, the button on my trousers was unfastened, and I tensed up as the zipper was lowered. Obviously, this wasn't the first time Amelia had stripped me out of my clothes. But it was the first time with an audience.

I heard a squeak from the shower, and glanced across to see Ed leaning back against Coren, his eyes closed once again as his cock slid gently between Coren's fingers, soap bubbles making the delicate skin slick, glistening in his pubic hair, pearling like precum at the tip of his exposed head.

My mind wandered as Amelia grabbed the waistband of my trousers along with the waistband of my boxers underneath, and started pulling them down. I couldn't see Coren's cock. The way Ed

14

was moaning, the way he was moving up and down as he leaned back against the ocean of solid muscle that was Coren's body, I couldn't help but imagine-

"Oh, fuck," I moaned, biting my lip painfully as Amelia's lips slid gently over the head of my cock, her tongue lapping playfully at the tip. "Shi---t." I absently gripped her hair, but she pulled away.

She smacked my ass playfully as she stood, then kissed my lips. "Now, go play, Coren's waiting."

I met Coren's eyes and he smirked as he leaned in to gently bite Ed's ear, making him yelp and squirm.

"What do you think of his package?" Coren asked, his voice a stage whisper, barely audible over the rush of the water. "You like what you see?"

My heart thundered as I stepped toward the shower. I'd never done anything like this before, but Coren and Ed were good looking guys. And they were my friends. They'd go slowly with me.

Ed nodded as my cock bounced up and down. On a moan, he said, "I like it."

"Good boy," said Coren. "I want you to suck him off."

My head went light as I stepped into the shower. All eyes were on me. I was the centre of attention. And I was about to be thrown in at the deep end.

Chapter 8

Ed

Hugh paused, and I could see his mind working behind his eyes. Had he just heard Coren right? He looked me up and down, but my own eyes settled on his crotch.

His cock was already half-erect. Already glistening with Amelia's spittle. Thoughts tumbled in my mind. Was I really going to do this? With an audience as well? What if he came in my mouth? The thought was at once exhilarating and nerve wracking. What would it taste like? What would it feel like in my mouth? Running down my throat?

"Chop chop," Coren said, and I could hear the amusement in his voice. "This one is getting restless."

He grabbed my cock firmly in his fist and slid the skin over the hardness beneath. It was painful. It was wonderful. I cried out and gasped and almost lost consciousness, my eyes drifting closed of their own accord as the heat of the water had me falling.

When I felt Coren's teeth score the skin of my shoulder, I jerked awake fast. And there, right in front of me, was Hugh.

His gaze wandered over my face before he met my eyes square. "You don't have to--"

"I--ahhhh--" Coren's hand slid between my buttocks, a finger putting pressure on my anus. For a moment, I lost my train of thought, lost track of everything except the sensation as I rubbed myself against my friend. Up, and down, and up, and down, his fingertip just stimulating the nerve endings. "Fuck," I moaned, and noticed a look of insecurity pass over Hugh's face.

Hugh had never struck me as the nervous type. He was sporty, popular, easy going. But my heart almost broke when his face fell, when I sensed a change in energy, what you might call 'third-wheel-syndrome'. He didn't know if he should be there, if maybe he was surplus to requirements.

Nothing could have been further from the truth.

I licked my lips, then gently bent at the knees and lowered myself in front of him. Coren's hand trailed up from my ass, into the small of my back, then along to my shoulder blades as I crouched, then as I brought my head in line with Hugh's quivering dick, I gulped and savoured the moment.

Placing my hands gently on his thighs, I used my thumbs to massage his soft muscles. He wasn't as solid as Coren, but there was strength beneath the skin. Pulling it apart flattened the skin at his pelvis, pulling his ball sack tight and making his cock look longer, more enticing even than it had been. Trimmed pubic hair had been shaped in a gentle arch above his shaft, and I stroked my thumbs through it.

When I took him into my mouth, I heard the roar escape his lips, only for it to be cut off quickly by what I could only assume was Coren's mouth.

Chapter 9

Ed

Hugh's cock tasted bitter with Amelia's spit. It filled my mouth and I sucked gently, letting my tongue glide along the underside, feeling the ridges of veins that stood out along the shaft. His foreskin shifted back as he grew harder, larger, and I felt the head start to press at the back of my throat as I leaned in, taking as much as I could.

My lips moved over the soft skin, and as I gently sucked on him I used my hands to twist and squeeze the shaft, to cup his balls and roll them through my fingers.

Hugh's high-pitched squeals and low moans drove me on, drove me to take more, to use my tongue to swirl around his cock, over the head, feeling the heat grow inside my mouth.

A smack of air as their kiss broke, Hugh's gasped breath. "Fuck, I can't-"

"Oh, we've only just started," Coren said, letting out a low chortle. "You can hold out, Hugh, otherwise Amelia's going to think she's doing something wrong."

"Jesus."

I felt Hugh's fingers twist into my hair, pulling my head forward over his shaft and holding me there, cock filling my mouth like a gag. For a moment, I thought I might choke, then I remembered to breathe through my nose, scents of sex and soap suds.

"Oh, God..." Amelia's words were a reflex, a muttered interjection meant only for herself. I glanced across to see her leaning against the door frame, eyes fixed firmly on the three of us as her hand moved at her crotch.

When Hugh released his grip on my head, I gratefully moved back, letting his dick drop from my mouth and taking a deep, quivering breath as the hot water splashed against my back. But I wasn't ready to give him a moment to recover. I wanted him riding the edge, unable to think clearly. I grabbed his red, throbbing cock in both hands, twisting the base as I stroked the head.

Slow. Stop. Fast.

He gasped and panted, bleated high squeaks and moaned long, low growls. He fell hard against the shower wall, his feet slipping against the floor, but stayed upright as I played with him. My own cock strained at full stretch, ready for any stimulation, but not ready for Coren's next move.

I felt him crouch behind me, ticklish fingers trailing down the sides of my back as he leaned forward. Pressure at my ass felt like fingers, but I knew that his hands were clutching at my flesh, thumbs pressing hard into my hips, sending flashes of pure pleasure into my brain.

"Do you want me inside you?" His words were whispered directly into my ear. "Your choice, Ed, we can save it for next time."

I gasped, losing my concentration. Next time. The confidence in his voice, knowing that this wouldn't be the last time we enjoyed each other's company like this... It was such a turn on. Involuntarily, I squeezed my pelvic muscles, immediately wishing I hadn't as my orgasm threatened to fall over the edge.

"Oh fuck," I gasped, squealing against the tide. "Oh, fuck, fuck, fuck..."

"Do you want it, Ed?"

I nodded, squeezing my eyes shut, forcing myself to relax as I anticipated this newest sensation.

Chapter 10

Ed

Leaving Hugh's cock twitching and jumping, riding the edge of orgasm, I turned around to see Coren tearing open a foil packet with his teeth. The condom had come from nowhere, it would seem, and the suspicion dawned on me that perhaps all this hadn't been entirely accidental. Had I been intended to find him in the shower? Had he known that I would be turned on by it? What exactly did that mean?

More importantly, how did I feel about it? Was it creepy or did it only serve to excite me more?

One thing was certain, I was enjoying myself too much to stop.

I moved into a kneeling position, letting the shower water soak my head as I gasped and spluttered beneath it. Grabbing Coren's thick cock with one hand, I ran a thumb along the underside, stimulating it, hardening it, before kissing the tip and letting my lips glide over the shaft.

"Oh, we are getting used to our new place in the world, aren't we, Ed?"

I tilted my head back, letting my eyes drift up along his rippling torso, hard pectorals glistening with soap and water, and met his gaze looking down. Grasping his thighs with both hands, I pulled myself up, keeping his cock in my mouth for as long as I could before it came free, then grabbed the condom out of his hands as I stood, slipping it from the packet.

"How did you know?"

"Some things are better kept secret. Do you mind?"

I shook my head, pinching the tip of the condom and gently rolling it over his shaft. "I guess not. Coren, I've never had anything inside me."

His hand went to my face, brushing a cheek, fingers curling over my ear. "Nervous?"

I nodded.

"Just relax. If you don't like it, we can stop. You're in charge, Ed, I would never ever do anything to hurt you."

His eyes met mine, and I saw both concern and compassion in them. Coren was letting me have the leash, and it was exactly what I needed. All the control he'd exercised over me before had gone. He wanted me to know that I could take this fast, or I could take it slow, and if we'd already gone far enough then he wouldn't push.

"OK," I said, nodding. "Just be gentle, yeah?"

"Always."

Having Hugh and Amelia there felt safer. Their presence let me experiment comfortably. I ran nervous fingers down over Coren's pelvis, around his cock, cupping his balls, and we came together for a soft, gentle kiss.

Then, satisfied, I lowered myself down, turned, and gabbed Hugh's waist.

"I want that cock back in my mouth," I said, and saw it twitch in anticipation.

Getting down on all fours as Hugh tried to move into a sitting position on the bottom of the shower would have been comical if it wasn't so sexy. In the small space we were pushed close together, but I took every opportunity to lick the head of Hugh's cock or get my lips around it for a quick kiss.

Then, as we finally moved into position, his dick right in front of my face where I wanted it, myself crouched low with my ass in the air, I felt Coren moving behind me, getting ready.

And as I wrapped my lips around Hugh's throbbing cock, I felt the pressure of Coren's pressing against my tight, virgin hole.

Chapter 11

Ed

"How does that feel?" Coren grabbed a handful of my hair and tugged it back as he whispered into my ear, but that wasn't what he was talking about.

I let Hugh's cock fall from my mouth, watching the red, swollen head twitch and spasm as he rode the edge of an orgasm that was just waiting to explode into my throat. A deep breath filled my lungs and I rocked my hips, letting Coren's cock slide up and down between my buttocks. "When are you going to put it in me?"

Coren laughed. "Patience, Ed. You're tight. You need to relax your anus, let the muscles go loose." He ran a finger down my back, rocking me with a shiver that seemed to emanate from my feet. "Can you do that for me?"

I took a deep breath, then leaned further forward, ignoring the pain as his fingers pulled on my hair. A quick nod, and I let my muscles sag, feeling the tension release in my pelvis, my ass, my cock, even my thighs. It was an odd sensation, a moment of relaxation like meditation mixed with a feeling of tingling anticipation not unlike being ready to pee. I put my mouth back on Hugh's cock and heard him bleat as I nibbled gently at the head, bringing him back to the edge.

And then I felt it. Coren's cock pressed against my back passage, stretching my hole wider as it delved just inside. My mind exploded with new sensation, the nerve endings there suddenly pulsing at the stimulation. I knew that this was naughty, taboo. Coren was my friend, Hugh too, and the fact that Amelia was there watching...

A quiver passed through my body and I rolled my back, undulating against Coren's cock as I sucked at Hugh, taking his shaft deeper, revelling in the feeling of being filled from both ends.

Coren grunted, then leaned close to my ear and whispered: "It's going deeper. Can you feel that, Ed?"

I nodded, unable to talk, relaxing further and letting his cock slide inside my ass.

"Ohh, fuck, that feels good." Coren let out a quivering sigh as his dick went deeper.

A sudden spark of pleasure lit up my brain as he came into contact with my prostate. I opened my mouth wide, ready to emit a scream of need, then gagged as the head of Hugh's cock filled my throat. I pulled back instinctively, but that only served to push Coren's cock deeper into my ass, rubbing his shaft against my prostate and setting off pulses through my spine that made me shudder and almost collapse.

Coren was panting behind me, one hand wrapped into my hair as the other slid around my waist, then lower, finding my cock hard and needy. The touch of his fingers made me tense and he cried out, pulling back, his cock pulsing inside me, filling me, making me almost black out.

I took Hugh back into my mouth as I fell into rhythm with Coren, moving forward and back against them both. Hugh undulated and arched, and I felt his temperature change against my tongue.

Then, almost without warning, he exploded into my mouth.

Chapter 12

Ed

Hugh's cum hit the back of my throat, warm and sticky. His cock spasmed a second time and I felt the whole of my mouth fill with the fluid. Gloopy, stringy semen trickled down my tongue and I closed my eyes at the salty, tangy flavour. This was such a new sensation, and I wanted to enjoy it. Even as he continued to burst inside my mouth, I moved my head up and down his shaft, squeezing my lips tight to hold it inside as I milked every last drop from his tip, sucking as hard as I could.

"Fuuuck..." Hugh groaned and wriggled against the floor of the shower, hands slapping into the water pooled there as he tried to find purchase, tried to shift his body away from my continued sucking. "Ohhhh, fuck..."

As I sucked, Coren increased the tempo of his thrusting, moving his cock in and out of my ass, brushing the head again and again against my prostate, stimulating it over and over, sending pulses of pleasure through every inch of my body. My own cock throbbed with need, hard and swollen as Coren's fingers moved up and down the shaft.

Hugh's dick finally started to soften, and I let it slide gently from my lips, listening to his panting slow, then quicken as I lapped one last time at his hole before letting him go. I spread the flavour of his cum around my mouth, revelled in it, then finally swallowed it back just as Coren started to rut into me with a fervour that could only mean he was close to the end.

"Give it to me, Coren," I screamed, panting as my body was thrown forward again and again.

Hugh was staring at me. "Fuck, did you just swallow all that?"

I nodded, a small smile spreading over my lips, then opened my mouth and wriggled my tongue to show him.

"So fucking tight," Coren moaned, his breath gasping in time with each thrust. "I'm close."

Lightning flashed through my brain and my cock spasmed as his head hit hard against my prostate. I squeezed my eyes shut, arching back and tensing through my whole body as it felt like I orgasmed without ejaculating. I cried out, my voice reverberating in the small space, mixing with Coren's grunts as he thrust harder, faster, again and again and started to scream with each movement.

The feeling when he finally came inside my ass was at once both satisfying and mind blowing. I felt heavy and full, the pressure increased but not uncomfortable. His cock pulsed inside me and I was no longer able to hold back. I bucked against Coren, jerking my head back and drawing in a quick, sharp breath as my own cock spasmed and I felt the cum shoot out onto the tiled floor.

"Oh, Jesus...Jesus..." Coren panted and moaned as he collapsed forward over me, his weight heavy against my back. "Oh, Jesus fucking Christ." The words were punctuated by a laugh and a sigh, then a heavy, relieved grunt, and I felt his cock slide from my ass. "That was fantastic," he whispered.

Amelia, almost fogotten at the other end of the bathroom, bleated and sighed. "You guys, that was so fucking hot."

I laughed, feeling the heat rise to my face. I couldn't believe what we'd just done together.

"Did you enjoy yourself?" Coren asked, his thumb rubbing my cheek.

I nodded. "Mmm."

Hugh leaned in, kissed Coren, then me, his face soaked with a mixture of sweat and water from the shower. "Perhaps we could do it again sometime?"

Coren laughed. "Sure, I'm game. Ed?"

"Yes," I said, sighing as I shifted myself from beneath him, stretching my legs out to bring some feeling back into them. "Yes please."

Excerpt - Old Scores

Please enjoy the following excerpt from my gay Vampire erotic romance, Old Scores.

Scene 1

"Come home with me." I met Steadman's eyes, saw them dilate. The grin spread over his lips slowly, as if he was processing the idea. "I promise you'll enjoy it."

He slipped his fingers around the glass on the bar, caressing it, then lifted it to his lips. "I shouldn't, Vic."

"I think you should."

"It's against the rules." He took a sip, his dark eyes glued to mine. Rules. What did I care about rules? After a hundred and fifty years, they hardly mattered to me any more.

I held his gaze, let my hand trail across the bar and lightly touched his elbow. "Can't we bend the rules? Just this once?"

The smile pulled at the corner of his lips and he lowered his gaze. "I'm your lecturer, Vic. It just wouldn't be..."

Leaning in closer, I dropped my voice to a hoarse whisper. "It'll be our secret. You'd like that, wouldn't you?"

"I..." He shivered. I could see the battle raging inside him. "Come on."

My hand went to the inside of his thigh, my fingers spreading until they found resistance at his crotch. He moaned as I pushed the pants tighter around his cock, letting the shape of it form in the folds, watching, waiting for his reply.

His breathing was ragged, but he nodded. I took his hand and led him outside.

***

Scene 2

A car hummed by, tyres whooshing on the dry asphalt. People milled about, young students in short skirts, tight shirts, flirting and taking each other's hands as they led lovers to quiet corners or back to dorm rooms. Steadman kept himself apart from me, trying to avoid being spotted going home with one of his students. I hung an arm around his shoulders, pulled him closer.

The blood raged in my veins. My hard-on was thick and full, for sex and blood and the feel of a human life in my hands. My influence over him was only gentle, just lowering his inhibitions. I'd never had much of a talent for that. But keeping him close made him pliant, made him forget who he was and what he should be doing.

"Kiss me," I said, and pushed him to the wall of the bar. I leaned forward, he shook his head, but our lips met in any case. He was warm and welcoming, his lips damp and ready and willing. I pushed my tongue inside, tasted the alcohol in his saliva as he drew shallow breaths through his nose.

I wasn't the only one with a crush on Steadman Knowles. Boys, girls, I could tell by the way that their eyes lingered when they spoke to him, by the way that their minds went blank when he asked them the simplest of questions.

Thirty-two, dark hair, a sprinkling of beard. Easy to fall for.

A girl fell into us, knocking our lips apart, and I turned to find her struggling to tug herself away from two male police officers.

She spat at the shoes of one. "Hey, get off me!"

"Come on, miss."

"I said, get off me!"

I kept myself between the officers and Steadman as they wrestled the girl away from us. My abilities were never very developed, a result of my sire leaving as soon as I was turned, but invisibility was fairly simple. And if they didn't see me, they wouldn't see the gorgeous lecturer I was taking home.

"Is there someone who can come and fetch you?" One of the officers struggled to hold the girl steady while she bucked and screeched.

"I'm fine! I can get home on my own."

Steadman made a noise, about to tell them who she was. About to offer to get her home, naturally. He was a knight in shining armour, I already knew that. It was his personality as much as his looks that attracted me in the first place. But I was far more selfish.

I pressed a finger to his lips, caught one of the officers by the collar, leaned in to whisper in his ear. "Her name is Georgina." Her mind was leaking with intoxication, it wasn't difficult to find the name. "I think you should take her back to her apartment. Her roommate will be there already."

He didn't see me, of course. All he or his partner would remember was the girl.

"Georgina, calm down." The officer said, and she stopped struggling at the sound of her name. "We'll take you back to your apartment, right Gerry?"

I leaned back in for another kiss, desperate for the warmth that Steadman could provide, forgetting the interruption already. I pulled up close to his face, took in his scent, nipped at his chin. Then I moved down to his throat and felt his pulse through my lips as I kissed and licked his flesh.

"I shouldn't," he said again.

"Oh, you should. You definitely should."

***

Scene 3

A shadow swayed in the breeze, watching from the rooftop, focusing on the single human heartbeat emanating from the couple. It had been a long time since he'd seen Victor. Too long. There were scores to be settled, things that needed to be said.

As the couple moved unseen down the street, the shadow followed.

Dear reader,

I hope you enjoyed reading this book as much as I enjoyed writing it!

I'd be grateful if you would consider leaving an honest review so that others can discover it too. By leaving a review, even if it's only a few words, you support my work and help to ensure that I keep writing more books. You can find more of my writing at my blog, www.niccihaydon.com. There are free stories, announcements, articles about writing and links to my other published work. Why not stop by and get a free email subscription?

Thanks for reading!

About Nicci Haydon

Nicci Haydon lives in rural England, where she spends most of her time writing. Her romantic fiction has appeared on websites, in anthologies, and in a variety of published books. A vast and ever expanding collection of work is available for free at her personal website at niccihaydon.com, where you will also find announcements of new releases, discount codes and giveaways.

Follow her on Twitter @NicciHaydon or on Facebook to connect with her growing community.

Printed in Great Britain
by Amazon

33410200R00020